The Fancy Friend

by Kim Kane

illustrated by Jon Davis

PICTURE WINDOW BOOKS

a capstone imprint

For my dear friends Alice and Ness and their gorgeous Islas (who are not really like the Isla in this book). And for Martha, my 3-foot muse, to whom Ginger owes every ounce of her vim.

— Kim

Ginger Green is published by Picture Window Books,
A Capstone Imprint
1710 Roe Crest Drive
North Mankato, Minnesota 56003
www.mycapstone.com

Ginger Green, Playdate Queen — *The Fancy Friend*
Text Copyright © 2016 Kim Kane
Illustration Copyright © 2016 Jon Davis
Series Design Copyright © 2016 Hardie Grant Egmont
First published in Australia by Hardie Grant Egmont 2016

Library of Congress Cataloging-in-Publication Data
is available on the Library of Congress website.

978-1-5158-1948-6 (library binding)
978-1-5158-1954-7 (paperback)
978-1-5158-2016-1 (eBook PDF)
978-1-5158-2034-5 (reflowable epub)

Summary: Today, Ginger is having a playdate with Isla. But Isla won't share! That's not fun. How will Ginger solve this problem?

Designers: Mack Lopez and Russell Griesmer
Production specialist: Laura Manthe

Printed and bound in China.
010737S18

Table of Contents

Chapter One.................................. 7

Chapter Two 33

Chapter Three............................ 51

Chapter
One

My name is Ginger Green.

I am seven years old.

I am the Playdate Queen!

Yesterday, Isla called.

She said, "Hello, Ginger Green,
Playdate Queen. Would you like
to come over and see my room?"

I said,

"YES!"

Isla lives on the other side
of the highway, near the river.

Isla is my friend from school.
Even though Isla is in a different
class, we play together at lunch
and recess.

Mom and
I arrive at
Isla's house.

Isla's house is **BIG** and white.
I ring the doorbell. It is silver.
There is a camera next to the door

"Fancy,"

I say.

I knew Isla's house would be fancy. Even Isla's name is fancy because you don't say the "s."

Isla's mom opens the door.

The door is very TALL.

Isla's mom is very TALL.

She smiles.

Mom squeezes my hand.
"Bye," she says.

"See you in two hours."

I walk inside.

The house is quiet.

Isla comes down the stairs.
She is not wearing shoes.
She is wearing fancy slippers.

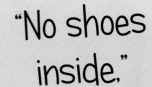

"No shoes inside,"

says Isla.

I take off my boots.

I follow Isla up to her bedroom.

Her room is big.

Her room is purple.

Her room is
fancy and clean.

There is a big purple rug.

There is a purple chair. There is a big purple bed. There is even a swing. **In the bedroom!**

I **run** to the swing.

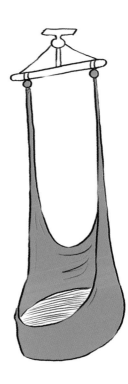

"DON'T RUN!"

says Isla.

"No running in the house."

I stop.

"And DON'T touch my swing," says Isla.

"Why not?"

I ask.

"The swing is special," says Isla.

"I will be careful," I say.

"The swing is only
for **ME**," says Isla.

"Oh,"

I say.

I love swings.

Isla gets on the swing.

She SWINGS and SWINGS.

Then she JUMPS and lands on the bed. Isla JUMPS up and down on the bed.

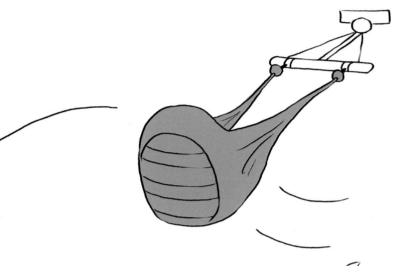

It looks

fun.

I jump up on
the bed too.

The bed is soft. The bed is bouncy.
I love jumping.

Isla stops jumping.

"This is **MY** bed," she says.
"Only I can jump on it."

"Oh,"

I say.

I get down.

I feel small.
I feel sad.

Chapter Two

Isla starts jumping on her big purple bed again.

Then I see the dolls.

Isla has a bookshelf full of dolls.

There are baby dolls and big girl dolls. There are wooden dolls and china dolls and rock star dolls.

Isla's bookshelf is like a doll shop.

"Wow," I say. "You have so many dolls."

"I know," says Isla. "I love dolls."

"I love dolls too!"

I say.

I pick up a baby doll. Isla has five baby strollers. I count them. I put the baby doll in one of the strollers.

Isla takes the stroller from me.

"That is **MY** doll," she says.

"This doll is **NOT** for you."

I pick up another baby doll.

"That is my
doll too,"

says Isla.

Isla has one baby doll in her hand. She has one baby doll in the stroller.

I reach for another doll.

"STOP!"

says Isla.

I stop.

I am Ginger Green, Playdate
Queen. I love playdates. And
on playdates you have to
share. That is the rule.

"You have to share your toys,"
I say to Isla. "That is the rule."

"I don't want you touching my stuff. I don't like anyone touching my stuff. I invited you over to **see** my room. I did not invite you over to **touch** it," says Isla.

Isla is making me

MAD.

This is **NOT** a playdate.
On a playdate you
have to play.

I walk to the door.

"STOP!"

says Isla.

I don't stop.
I am too mad.
I walk out of the purple room.

"STOP!" says Isla.

I still don't stop. **I am still too mad**. I walk to the top of the white stairs.

"STOP!"

says Isla again.

I stop. I turn around. Isla
is holding out a doll. It is
a doll I don't like.

It is a doll with only one eye.
It is a doll with only one arm.

"You can play with **this** one," says Isla.

"Thank you," I say. "But **you** can keep that one."

Chapter
Three

Isla looks sad.

She holds the doll tight.

"I would like to choose my own doll."

I say.

"OK," says Isla in a quiet voice.

Isla does not know the rules, but she is kind. I can teach my friend Isla.

We walk back into Isla's purple room. We walk over to the dolls.

I pick up a baby doll.

Isla does not say **NO**.

Isla nods.

I am Ginger Green, Playdate Queen. I can teach Isla the rules. That is what Playdate Queens are for.

At four o'clock, the doorbell rings.

DING DONG!

Mom comes up the stairs
with Isla's mom. I don't want
to go home.

"They have played so well,"
says Isla's mom. "I haven't
heard a peep."

"Did you have fun?"
Mom asks me.

"Oh, yes,"

I say.

"Oh, yes,"
says Isla.

"Would you like to come to
our house one day?" I ask.

Isla smiles. "I have never been on a playdate at someone else's house."

"Well," I say, "come over soon!"

I am Ginger Green, Playdate Queen, and I know you must always return a favor.

I want Isla to come to my house but not just because that is the rule. I want Isla to come over because she is my friend.

We both LOVE dolls.

We both LOVE swings.

We both LOVE jumping.

And now we BOTH
know the rules!

THE END

About the Author

Kim Kane

Kim Kane is an award-winning author who writes for children and teens in Australia and overseas. Kim's books include the CBCA short-listed picture book *Family Forest* and her middle-grade novel *Pip: the Story of Olive*. Kim lives with her family in Melbourne, Australia, and writes whenever and wherever she can.